JOSHUA Drusor

CAP'N SMUDGE

Written By:
STEPHEN COSGROVE

Illustrated By:
ROBIN JAMES

A Serendipity Book

Printed in U.S.A.

ISBN #0-915396-17-3 CAP'N SMUDGE

Dedicated to Jennifer and Julie, through whose eyes I see most of the world.

S. Cosgrove

On a beat up, battered boat in a very small port, on a very small island, in a very, very small sea, stood the dirtiest, dustiest sea captain in the world. He had gum wrappers stuck in his hair, coal dust on his nose, a filthy smile on his face and instead of a parrot on his shoulder he had a muddy, mucky mudlark. He was so dirty and despicable that he didn't even have a real wooden leg but instead used an old mop handle with the mop still hooked on the end.

None of the other sailors or the fishermen who lived in the port knew his name but they called him Cap'n Smudge.

Now, Smudge hadn't always been like this. In fact, he once was a normal, healthy person like you or me. But one day, while rowing far out into the bay, where his father had told him never to go, his boat was capsized by a large and fairly ferocious sea monster who, unfortunately, and quite accidentally, bit off his leg.

Even then things would have been all right, for a friendly carpenter in town carved him a wooden leg that was just as good as the old one. But the other fishermen who lived in town made fun of him. They teased and teased, calling him "Peg Leg" and "Old Wooden Toes" and one day they even set fire to his artificial leg.

Fortunately, he was able to put the fire out by dousing it in a rain barrel, but alas, the wooden leg was damaged beyond repair.

Being the poor fisherman that he was, he couldn't afford to buy another wooden leg so he fashioned one out of an old mop handle, thinking that it would just have to do.

Well, this did nothing to help the situation and the other fishermen just kept on teasing and teasing until Smudge vowed to get revenge.

Smudge thought and thought of ways to get even with all the people that had laughed at him and as he was thinking he accidentally dropped a candy wrapper in the water. He watched as it floated gently out to sea and there it got caught in the net of one of the fishermen. Well, everybody knows that you can't catch fish with paper stuck in your net, so, the fisherman pulled his net out of the water and removed the candy wrapper.

"Aha!" said Smudge, with a sly smile. "I know what I'll do to get even. I'll throw garbage and junk into the sea and then we'll see who laughs last!"

Smudge set about diligently picking up the garbage all over the town and stuffing it in an old dirty bag. He picked up tin cans, old pans, garbage cans and anything that looked like junk. Then he dragged it down to the bay and threw it all in the sea.

"That'll teach you to laugh at me!" he shouted. And with that, he went to find some more.

And so it went on for years and years: Smudge steaming by in his beat up old boat, throwing garbage and junk merrily over the side and the fishermen constantly cleaning their nets.

Finally, out of frustration, all the fishermen decided to hold a mass meeting to find a solution to their problem.

They all gathered on the port side of the dock on the bay. There were Robert McJames, the tuna fisherman, Large Marge, Sarge of the Barge, who was always fishing for crab, and all the rest of the fishermen who worked on the sea.

"What are we going to do?" they cried. "Smudge has thrown so much garbage in the water that the fish won't even swim near our nets."

Old Marge cleared her voice, which was something like a foghorn, and said, "If I remember right, there is a creature that sails the seas who helps folks like you and me, and her name is Serendipity. Surely if we can find her, she can solve the problem of what to do about grundgy old Smudge."

With no other choices before them, they set out to find Serendipity.

Suddenly, off to the starboard appeared the biggest, pinkest sea serpent you have ever seen. Marge shouted, "Are you Serendipity?"

Serendipity smiled a very shy smile and nodded her head.

"Well," said Marge, "We've really got a problem." And with that she told Serendipity all about Cap'n Smudge and his evil, smelly ways. When Marge was through telling the tale, Serendipity thought for just a moment and then quickly set off in search of Smudge to talk to him about the problem.

She had been looking for a long, long time when suddenly she saw a large, black, oily cloud moving toward her at a very fast rate. "Aha!" she thought, "This must be Smudge now. When he gets here I'll talk to him about the problem and show him the error of his ways."

She cleared her throat and said, "Ahem, Mr. Smudge, I would like to talk to you for just a minute, if I could." But old Smudge didn't even slow his boat down one little bit and just steamed on by. And if that wasn't enough, he threw a whole can full of garbage right on Serendipity's head.

Now Serendipity was mad. All she had wanted to do was discuss the problem. But, instead Smudge had thrown garbage on her.

Using all the speed she could muster, Serendipity chased after the dirty old boat. It took a bit of doing but she finally caught him by running his boat up onto the beach.

"Okay, Cap'n Smudge," she said, "Now what's with all this garbage you're throwing in the water?"

Smudge sadly told her the whole story. When he had finished, there was a large tear in Serendipity's eye. With a lump in her throat, she swam quickly back to the port.

Serendipity called all the fishermen together and told them what had happened. When she had finished, all the fishermen hung their heads in shame.

"But what can we do?" they asked. Serendipity thought for a moment and then came up with a marvelous plan. Quickly she told the fishermen and they all agreed, then hurried off to set the plan in action, while Serendipity set off to pull Cap'n Smudge and his boat off the beach.

By securing a heavy rope around her neck, she was able to pull Smudge and his boat safely back to the harbor where all the fishermen were waiting with smiles from ear to ear.

"Smudge!" said Large Marge when he was safely standing on the dock, "Serendipity has told us that the only reason you're so mean and spiteful is 'cause we don't love you and made fun of your wooden leg. So, we all got together and made you a brand new one." And with that, she presented Cap'n Smudge with the most beautifully carved wooden leg you have ever seen.

With large, muddy tears in his eyes, Smudge gratefully accepted the gift, and hugged each of his new friends, promising never to throw garbage in the water again.

SO IF YOU EVER SEE SOMEONE
DIFFERENT THAN YOU OR ME
JUST REMEMBER CAP'N SMUDGE
AND THIS TALE OF SERENDIPITY.